The rights of Sandra Horn and Ken Brown to be identified as the author and illustrator of this work have been asserted
by them in accordance with the Copyright, Designs and Patents Act, 1988.
First published in Great Britain in 1995 by Andersen Press Ltd., 20 Vauxhall Bridge Road, London SW1V 2SA.  Published
in Australia by Random House Australia Pty., 20 Alfred Street, Milsons Point, Sydney, NSW 2061.  All rights reserved.
Colour separated in Switzerland by Photolitho AG, Offsetreproduktionen, Gossau, Zürich.  Printed and bound in Italy
by Grafiche AZ, Verona.

10   9   8   7   6   5   4   3   2   1

British Library Cataloguing in Publication Data available.

ISBN  0 86264 596 4

*This book has been printed on acid-free paper*

# TATTYBOGLE

## By Sandra Horn
## Illustrated by Ken Brown

Andersen Press • London

Old Tattybogle stood in the middle of the field.  He had been there for a long, long time.  He was made of sticks and sacks and the farmer's worn-out clothes.  His head was full of straw and cheerful thoughts.

When the wind blew, he rocked from side to side and his hat jumped up and down, but it never blew away because it was tied under his chin with good strong twine.

"I like a bit of a dance," said Tattybogle.

When it rained, the drops made a drumming noise on his hat.
"Music!" said Tattybogle.  Little waterfalls ran down from his
floppy hat past his face.  He liked that.
"It's like being a statue in a fountain," said Tattybogle.

He was happy when the stars twinkled and the moon
shone.  Sometimes, when the nights were cold, ice-drops
glimmered in the sky, high up among the stars. Tattybogle
thought they were as pretty as a summerday rainbow.

He was happy when the snow made a mound on the top of his hat.

"It keeps my brains warm," said Tattybogle. "I feel just like a king with a silver crown."

One autumn day, the wind got up and began to blow very hard.

"Good stuff!" said Tattybogle. But the wind blew harder and harder and louder. Tattybogle was rocked about so much that he felt quite dizzy.

"Steady on," he said, "that's enough." But still the wind grew stronger. It howled like a pack of wolves, tearing leaves and branches from the trees. It snatched some of Tattybogle's stuffing and scattered it all along the hedge.

"Whoops!" said Tattybogle, as the top of his hat broke off and his scarf blew away.

"Ooh, no!" he said as he spun round twice and his coat buttons were ripped off.

"Help!" he cried as the wolfwind picked him up and tossed him into the hedge. His coat and trousers were torn away, and his stuffing was thrown into the air.

"Deary me," said Tattybogle, "all that's left of me is a stick and a few wisps of straw. I hope the farmer will find me soon and mend me."

But when the farmer came walking through his fields, he said, "Bless my soul, the wind has blown Tattybogle all to bits. His coat's in the ditch and his scarf's all tangled up in a holly bush. I wonder where the rest of him is. What's that? Oh, it's only an old stick." Then he went away again.

"Well," said the stick. "I can't be a Tattybogle without any stuffing or clothes. What else can I be?"

He tried to think, but he couldn't. He was just a stick.

Winter came, dark and cold.  First it rained, and the stick
sank a little way into the wet earth.  Then it froze, and the
stick was held fast in the icy ground.  Snow fell, making a
deep white carpet all over the earth.  It piled up round the
bottom of the old stick in the hedge.

The winter lasted a long time, and the stick stood there,
silent and still.  The moon shone bright across the field, but
no light fell on the old frozen stick in the dark corner of the
hedge.

One morning, there was a faint smudge of blue in the sky. The frost began to crack and melt. The snow turned to watery drops and rolled away. The sun crept out from behind a cloud and shone on the old stick.

Spring had come.

Slowly, a warm feeling spread through the stick. It started at the bottom and crept all the way up to the top. Then, tiny white buds began to grow under the ground.

The stick was growing roots.

The roots grew fast and deep. Near the top of the stick, where the sun shone warmest, more buds grew. They reached up towards the sky.

The stick was growing branches.

As the warm days went on, leaf-buds formed. Then it rained and the buds unfolded and opened. The new leaves fluttered in the air. A thin whispery voice from somewhere deep inside the stick said, "A drop of rain does you a power of good." Raindrops pattered on the new leaves.

"Music," said the voice.

The spring days grew longer and the sun shone.

New buds grew and broke into dancing golden catkins.

Then, one sunny morning, the farmer came with a bundle of sticks and straw and worn-out clothes. Tattybogle watched as he built a fine new scarecrow.

The new scarecrow looked across at Tattybogle.
"What a beautiful tree," he said.
"I feel like a king with a golden crown," said Tattybogle as he
waved his branches in the summer breeze.